WONDER WOMAN™
PERSEVERES

written by
CHRISTOPHER HARBO

illustrated by
GREGG SCHIGIEL

WONDER WOMAN created by
William Moulton Marston

PICTURE WINDOW BOOKS
a capstone imprint

Wonder Woman perseveres. She always works hard, and she never quits. She keeps people safe no matter what it takes.

When the Amazon Princess takes on a challenge, she gives it her all.

Wonder Woman perseveres by always
doing her best.

When the Amazon warrior hits a roadblock, she figures out a way around it.

Wonder Woman perseveres by thinking up
creative ways to solve problems.

When Wonder Woman is outnumbered, she doubles her efforts.

The Amazon Princess perseveres
by refusing to back down.

When Wonder Woman gets knocked down,
she gets right back up.

The Amazon warrior perseveres by dusting herself off and trying again.

When Wonder Woman gets in a bind, she taps into her strengths.

Wonder Woman perseveres by using her talents.

When Wonder Woman has a setback, she thinks about why it happened.

Wonder Woman perseveres
by learning from her mistakes.

When a task takes time, Wonder Woman sticks with it.

Wonder Woman perseveres by finishing
what she starts.

When the going gets tough, Wonder Woman uses sheer grit.

The Amazon warrior perseveres by working as hard as she can.

When Wonder Woman joins the fight,
everyone can count on her to do her job.

For no matter what, Wonder Woman
always perseveres!

WONDER WOMAN SAYS...

- Perseverance means giving your all, like when I push for the finish line while racing my Amazon sisters.

- Perseverance means solving your problems, like when I find a way around Giganta's roadblock.

- Perseverance means trying again when you fail, like when I get back up after Gorilla Grodd knocks me down.

- Perseverance means using grit, like when I go toe-to-toe with Devastation.

- Perseverance means being the very best you that you can be!

GLOSSARY

challenge (CHAL-uhnj)—something that is hard to do

creative (kree-AY-tive)—having to do with using your imagination to think up new ideas

grit (GRIT)—the ability to keep doing something even though it is very difficult

setback (SET-back)—something that delays you or keeps you from making progress

talent (TAL-uhnt)—something that you can do well and are good at

task (TASK)—a job that needs to be done

READ MORE

Pettiford, Rebecca. *Showing Perseverance.* Building Character. Minneapolis: Jump! Inc., 2018.

Schuh, Mari C. *Yes I Can!: A Story of Grit.* Stories with Character. Minneapolis: Millbrook Press, 2018.

Welbourn, Shannon. *Step Forward with Grit.* Step Forward. New York: Crabtree Publishing Company, 2017.

INTERNET SITES

FactHound offers a safe, fun way to find Internet sites related to this book. All of the sites on FactHound have been researched by our staff.

Here's all you do:

Visit *www.facthound.com*

Type in this code: 9781515840213

23

DC Super Heroes Character Education
is published by Picture Window Books
A Capstone Imprint
1710 Roe Crest Drive
North Mankato, Minnesota 56003
www.mycapstone.com

STAR41227

Editor: Julie Gassman
Designer: Charmaine Whitman
Art Director: Hilary Wacholz
Colorist: Rex Lokus

Cataloging-in-Publication Data is available
on the Library of Congress website.

ISBN: 978-1-5158-4021-3 (library binding)
ISBN: 978-1-5158-4288-0 (paperback)
ISBN: 978-1-5158-4025-1 (eBook PDF)

Printed and bound in the USA.
PA49